DIARY OF A LOST
BLACK QUEEN

*A Journey
to Finding
Her Crown*

by Destiny Kimble

ISBN – 978-1-5136-9640-9 (Paperback)

Publisher: Destiny Kimble

Cover image: Adobe Stock

Library of Congress Cataloging-in-Publication Data is available through the Library of Congress

#DiaryofaLostBlackQueen

This book is dedicated to my three precious daughters Londyn, Milan and Sierra-

If he can't buy you a simple ice cream cone

You may want to go ahead and leave him alone ☺

Love,
Mama

LOVE-
Bears all things
Believes all things
Hopes all things
Endures all things
Love never fails
-1 Corinthians 13:7

Life

Someone once said that love and life to them is family, doing laundry, and paying bills and taxes. Though family is life, the other things are not living. Living is to bring your family on to beautiful and amazing things. To see the world with them before you die. To take in all the structures, but more so the nature. Not just in one or two places, but in as many as you can. I have always felt this way. I read a great book entitled *The Alchemist* by Paulo Coelho. What I took away from it is that to work on something you don't love is to betray your heart. After my recent experiences, I now know that to betray your heart is to die.

It's been quite a few years. The past few years– hell the past 35 years or so, have not been all too kind to me. My name is Nile, and I am now of the ripe age of 38. I was not too kind to myself, but by adding the anguish from others, well, life started to become unbearable, to say the least. I would tell you why, but I don't even know where to begin.

What I do know is that I am driving from Colorado to California today by myself. The city of Lost Angels. I will document my trip with pictures and writing. I will attempt not to take any heartache along the way. I am staying on Venice Beach. I am so excited, I am nervous, but I am content with my heart intact. When you hit rock bottom in life, sometimes that is all you can ask for.

I feel that after everything, God had heard my prayers and my woes. I feel that I have been given a second chance at life. I have no money– well a little but not much, and I have no job. But I have been blessed with the means to have a very cute and romantic apartment for myself and my three girls, and I am blessed with enough funds to take this solo trip.

I have overpacked and my trip will be very short. From Colorado, it will be a 17-hour drive. I want to get there as soon as possible to smell the ocean and to get started on my journey. I have never traveled alone, and truth be told, I'm going there hoping to connect with a long-lost friend. One of the only true friends that I have ever had, but I don't think that will happen. So I am in for an adventure, and I plan to take in every second with gratitude and love.

I foresee tears of joy and heartache, but I know it is something that I must do. I feel compelled as if God himself heard me screaming, crying, and begging Him to please help me on the floor of my old bedroom when I hit the lowest point of my life. So, I will buckle up for the tears and joy. It is honestly the least I can do for God and myself.

It will be a solo trip, and by solo trip I mean myself along with God's presence. You see, I have no friends. Every friend I have had in my life either had ulterior motives or I lost them by being stupid or immature. I have my sister, whom I love dearly, but since we are night and day, sometimes it is hard to connect with her on an ultimate level. She is married, I am divorced. She is a homebody, and I now want to fly. Speaking of divorce, my girls tend to side more with my ex-husband at this point, and they had pretty much refused to come on this trip with me. Saying that he is my husband may be giving him too much credit, though, considering I never took his last name and we never actually filed for a marriage certificate.

My mom thinks it is a bad idea to drive over 17 hours by my-self as a single woman, but God says *go*. The people mentioned above are my hearts and they are closest that I have to what one would call a "friend," excluding Bernard, my ex.

I am not sure when I will arrive in Los Angeles– it will probably be around 2 am, which means it will be way too early for me to check into my room, but for some reason I don't care. I just want to get there. I will sleep in my car parked near the pier if need be. I only have from Wednesday to Sunday, and I intend to get the most out of it. I can sleep when I get back. I pray God gives me the energy to take it all in.

The things I look most forward to are listening to music on the way and eating (I will get more into my past eating habits to present later, but food has always been my favorite). I look for-ward to going to an art museum, eating at Mel's Drive-In on Sunset Boulevard, going to the ocean, watching the eclipse, and exploring. I have myself, my car, you, and my tunes. Getting in the shower. I will be back, Diary.

Well, hello again, it is now Friday and things have gone pretty much as expected. My drive here took longer than I thought it would. You'd think a 24-hour day is not much time, but it tends to go by very fast when you are working, going to lunch, doing hobbies, and then preparing dinner five days out of the week. Yet, driving by yourself with only music—geez, it felt like a much longer car drive than I had expected. I hope the trip back to Colorado is faster. People always say it is longer on your way somewhere, and shorter when you go back. I hope that is the case. My ass hurts from sitting on the seat for so long.

When I finally arrived after stopping in Vegas for an hour-long nap, I was approached by a homeless person on the beach. He did not look like he was anything but alive and hungry. He looked free as if he knew that somehow God would provide him a dollar to get his morning breakfast. He was unlike the home-less people I have encountered before in Colorado, looking for money to get their next fix. He looked free. He wore a dress and skated off on his skateboard after asking for a dollar. I had to pee very badly, so I felt it was an even exchange of gratitude—he told me where a public bathroom was, and I gave him a dol-lar for breakfast.

I was very anxious waiting for the sun to come up. The place I was staying at was not a normal hotel, but an apartment, and they were not open until 8:30 or so Pacific time. I slept a little bit in my car, but not much. When the sun came up, I could see the ocean on Venice beach, and I could hear the waves hitting the sand. The presence of the ocean was breathtaking. I smiled so much, a true smile, I felt so close to God. I felt humbled at the ocean's presence, even by the sand. I felt connected with it.

When I went back to my car, a man by the name of David knocked on my door to ask me if I was there to check in. I was parked in the check in spot, and he was doing his morning walk around the premises. I was so relieved to get my room. David was a black man, light skinned with blue or hazel eyes. As I waited for my room to be ready, we spoke about the injustices in life for black people and how it was not just due to our current president. He pointed out how this had been going on for a very long time. He talked about getting pulled over by police as a teen in Manhattan and just for driving a spiffy car. He talked about vices that his family dealt with and overall, I was able to see that the system we live in gives hope of one day being a better place, as in we can vote, we can do as much as we can, and maybe one day Trump or whoever the next racist president is will be overthrown. But I have now come to realize it has been this way for a long time. Sometimes, it feels like no matter who is leading it or running the show, as long as it is not a strong black man or woman, we will be in this system of control and unfairness forever. I am not racist, Diary. Just upset over injustices. Even with talking about such serious things, it was a peaceful conversation. The words David said rang true.

When we got to my room, I was overwhelmed with excitement. I always watched the movies or the magazines with these perfectly imperfect apartments or homes. Not too new, but with an old-world style. I have been obsessed with Paris and I am at early stages of learning French. *Comment* ça *va*, Diary. That means how are you doing. ☺ This apartment reminded me of a French apartment. David pointed out that it was actually Argentinian. It has French doors, hardwood floors, there is a sitting area/living room, and a cute kitchen that reminds me of something I would see on *Tiny Houses* on HGTV. It is quaint and perfect. The terrace is just phenomenal. There are plants and flowers, a table for two overlooking the pier that leads to the ocean. Though I am alone here, I wished in that moment that I could stay here forever. I fantasize about traveling back and forth between Colorado and California with my girls, living the best lives we can. I would stay in a place just like this. I would have two perfect homes in both states. I love to write, I have always loved to write, and this apartment on Venice beach was perfect for allowing me to do so.

The Fan

She's a writer at heart

She's just never gotten there

What she does oh what she does

Is listens to me

She listens with more than her ears

She listens with her heart

I need to paint you her shadow

I need to tell you her part

She is more than a fan

She is more than a musician

I can feel it in my pen

She is home and she is wishin'

That I was there with her

To sing and make her smile

I need my inspiration

She craves my inner style

I go to her...

She is covered in nothing but skin

We laugh we smoke we love

And when done I get my pen

I ask her to do what she loves

And so she starts to dance

This beautiful mighty fine lady

Had granted me one more chance

She is more than a fan

She is more than a musician

I can feel it in my tip

She is home and she is wishin'

That I was there with her

To sing and make her smile

I need my inspiration

She craves my inner style

Once I checked in, I went back out to the ocean as I waited for the cafe to open so that I could eat breakfast. I felt in bliss at this moment, I felt thankful, and I wrote in the sand the name of the man that I love with a heart next to it. He is the long-lost friend I am in hopes of reconnecting with. As soon as I did this, I looked to the right and there was the most beautiful rainbow that I have ever seen. I felt connected with God at that moment, and I felt connected to the man I love at that moment even though he was not there in the physical sense.

Needless to say, I was on cloud nine. I went into the cafe around 9:30 and ordered three egg whites with roasted potatoes. I recently changed my diet from eating anything and everything like bacon, steak, eggs over medium, and fish, to eating healthier. Some say you are what you eat for a reason, and I had not been feeling well for several years. I gave two cares less on what I ate for the most part. The man I love– we will call him X– told me once that we cannot be mad about a larger force feeding off us if we eat life forces smaller than us. It took a while for this to kick in, but once it did, it was as if the universe agreed and told me in my heart that I would not miss the meat. I have, needless to say—found all kinds of yummy vegan and organic food meals. I am working to incorporate this more into my daughters' diets as well. They don't quite like it yet.

A man sat next to me at the cafe. He sat with his back to me, but for some reason felt the need to try and have a conversation. He was a white man with a large build and blue eyes. He asked me a few questions about why I was here in California. I told him I drove straight through from Colorado to Vegas and then to California. He told me of some places I should go while in California, one of which was the Getty Museum. It was rainy and he said it would be a perfect day to go there. This was funny because I had planned on going there anyway, so I took this as a sign from God.

I went back to my room and got ready and was on my way. On the way there however, fear kicked in. I started seeing signs that my mind took in as negative, my fears telling me that I was all alone, that I shouldn't be here, that I was selfish, and that I may not make it back to my girls because I was all alone in a big city with no guide or friend. I was so scared that I called X twice just to go to his voicemail immediately. I was acting out of fear and was desperately missing him, and I really needed to hear his voice. The funny thing is, when I called him, I knew that he would not answer. The last time I spoke to him, I told him that I had heard his music on Spotify, that every song reminded me of him and I. I decided to keep the *every song reminded me about us* piece of the conversation out, but I think he knew that I felt this way. I told him that I was proud of him, but what I really wanted to say was *I love you so much, please let me be your friend again, please let me love you.* You can see why I was in hopes to connect with him as long of a shot as it was. I always give of myself, and too much at that... but for some reason, after listening to his music, I felt that he had been in a bad place with me for a long time.

He was very short with me when I spoke to him right before coming out to California. He said all of maybe ten words in total. It seemed as if he could not wait to hang up with me. He said he would call me back the night before I left to come here but he never did, and then here I go having a panic attack and desperately seeking X.

Ugh, it was pathetic as most women would agree. My message went something like this…"X, *please call me, please tell me what is going on… I am scared, please call me…*" Yeah, like I said… *ugh*! Even then, even after pure rejection, I still love him. Even knowing he may have cut me from his life completely, I still love him. I was so afraid that day that I left the museum immediately after paying for parking and my ticket. I did not go in.

I called my sister and told her I would be driving back home the next day. I had not even been in California for 24 hours. She told me to have a glass of wine and to come home if I felt like I was in danger. She made me laugh while I was crying. She told me to eat, drink, and love but then said, "*Oops, I think it is eat, pray, and love.*" I wanted a glass or five of wine, but something within me said *stay on your course, you can have wine later. I will take care of you*, the voice often said.

I was led to an organic nail salon that just so happened to offer the most amazing back massages. The lady that massaged me was very petite with small hands, yet they were so powerful. She gave the massages in ten-minute increments, and I just continued to ask for another 10 minutes. Even with having no money and having bills to pay, I felt like I was led there, and that money was not to be of concern at the moment. I could look for a job when I returned to Colorado.

After getting a massage and getting my nails done, I drove off and encountered a vegan restaurant around the corner. I ordered a margherita pizza and a salad. It was really good. I did not have wine, but I did have a really yummy green tea latte and water. I came back to the apartment very relaxed and very content even with the tragedies earlier in the day.

Thursday morning, I rose with an energy both healthful and good. I put on my headphones and ran on the beach. I felt like I was going to have a heart attack running at sea level, but I did it and I rewarded myself with a cup of coffee afterwards. I started thinking about a time when I was happiest outside of my hitting rock bottom. I was too thin then, but my hair was long and healthy, probably the only thing left that was healthy on me. After hitting rock bottom and going to a mental institution, yeah... we may or may not get more into that piece. I was diagnosed with bipolar disorder, and I had an experience I will never forget. Anyway, for some reason after I left there, I decided to chop off all my hair thinking it would grow back like it always had in the past. I was sorely mistaken, and not only did it not grow, it started to break off at every chance possible. It was as if my hair was even betraying me. I braided it in hopes that it would grow again but after two months in braids, it was only weaker and broke more- so I cut it all off with a little bang left in the front... almost like a mohawk.

I remember a phone call with X when we were laughing because I was giving him a hard time about working so closely with me on his music, but never supporting my pictures and posts like I saw him do with others. Now this seems silly looking back, but at the time, even though we were quote-un-quote just friends, I was jealous and wanted his attention and I couldn't just be honest with myself about it. Being with Bernard did not help. X must have felt badly about this conversation because he went through and liked all my recent posts and said he would love me with no edges and even if I had a mohawk. After my cup of coffee, I decided it was time for a California weave, my first real one, and on the way, I stopped at a local vegan Thai restaurant for lunch and ate by myself. It was very good.

For my hair, I went to a shop with an owner by the name of Gloria. She was very sweet and got me in touch with her stylist Tonya. Tonya and I sat alone in the shop listening to R&B as she braided my hair and sewed in my new weave. I would be lying if I told you that every song that played did not remind me of X. Some of them made me glow in thought of him, some of them made me sad, as if I had missed the chance of a lifetime to be with him. I mostly glowed. I especially glowed when *Overjoyed* by Stevie Wonder played. I have heard this song a few times in life, and I always loved it. I just never could recall the song to play it again. This was likely due to the fact that I could not relate it to anything or anyone throughout my years on earth. The words and the melody were so beautiful, and a few tears dropped from my eyes as I sat there getting my hair done that day.

Rush

I was always rushing, rushing, rushing

Never thinking twice

And I got myself to the point of rushing

Past the love of my life

I paid Tonya and thanked her, I called Gloria and thanked her as well. I told them that I would be back to get my weave maintained even though in my heart I wondered how I would ever be able to do so in my current financial situation. It was the dream or thought that counted in that moment.

I was looking kind of cute, but I knew it would be silly to go out to a nightclub in LA by myself, whether it was to let loose on my own or another desperate attempt to run into X, so I came home to my apartment and I remember an inner voice telling me to go outside. I saw people looking at the ocean, and so I too went back to the powerful source, and once again fell to my knees. When I say *fell to my knees*, I mean it in an emotional sense. A sense where you are compelled to cry, to cleanse, to get your innermost fears and thoughts out, your shames, your disgraces. I prayed and I asked that God have mercy on my soul for all of my past transgressions. I felt ashamed that I had only been near the ocean a few times in my life and that my girls weren't here with me, and that they had only taken in its beauty and power a few times, mainly with my ex-husband, who happens to be white. Please note, for the record, I am not racist. I have white in me. My grandma is German and white. She passed away at the age of 82, and ironically enough, she did so while I was here in California. I said my goodbyes as she lay in a hospice a couple days before leaving for this solo trip.

Egypt In Venice

After confiding in the ocean, I came up to a store that I had not seen before on the pier. I have always been fascinated with Egypt, and recently, before ending my marriage, I mentioned several times to Bernard that I wanted to go. He always said it was too violent of a place to go, but I still wanted to go, and even told him at one point, *"Then I would have to go by myself."* The store I encountered had oils, artwork, pipes, jewels, crystals, anything you could ever imagine, and it was all amazing to look upon. The beauty in this store alone was breathtaking, and a man by the name of Saber approached me and asked if I was there for a cleansing. He said he knew that I was and said he saw me go to the ocean. He asked if he could show me some things. The moment felt well, very enchanting. I told him I was looking for a ring. My inner mind told me I would know it when I saw it. I tried on several, but most were too big. Saber asked what my birth stone was. I told him I was born on November 24th and that I thought it was topaz. He said that is accurate, but then proceeded to give me a silver ring with a turquoise gem on two sides, and a deep purple stone in the middle. It is one of the most beautiful rings I have ever seen. He then began to speak about the chakras and started talking about the effects of lavender and two other oils used for sleep and scents. They smelled amazing, and I was hooked. The oils were about 65 dollars each, so I was now counting in my head how much this was all going to cost and had no clue that I was actually nowhere near done shopping. It was as if God had compelled me once again to meet this man and to not worry about the cost of the things He wanted to place in my life. Who can argue with God?

I then started looking at the crystals and saw many in the form of necklaces. I picked out a crystal necklace, but Saber said this was not the right one, and he picked out one that was even more stunning than the one I had. He changed the chain as he did not like it and helped me put it on. It is a white crystal with beautiful green and purple stones attached to it...almost in the form of a cross. It is stunning and he said it would protect me. The funny thing is, since moving out into my own place in Colorado and even while driving here, I have already felt protected. However, who will argue against further protection? I asked how much things were, and I came to a total of about $300.00... but we were not done. Now I needed a bracelet, and Saber suggested the protecting bracelet of Fatima and the chakra bracelet, which I broke a day later.

The bracelet of Fatima has gems encircling a small, silver-plated hand. It is like a very fancy charm bracelet, and I adore it already. Once done spoiling myself in jewels (at this point I was feeling like a princess), he said he wanted me to meet Adele, the man responsible for the amazing artwork that I saw everywhere in the store. There was a young teenage boy cleaning glass and working and I couldn't help but envy him in a way. He was with family, and he was around these amazing jewels and the breathtaking art that you would only expect to see in a very affluent art museum. Adele started to show me artwork in the $3,000 dollar range. The artwork showed ancient Egypt, and I remember my heart dropping because once again I knew I had no choice in the matter of obtaining and purchasing a piece of artwork. God said I must, and I promised myself that my heart was a part of God, and that I would no longer betray it. So, I braced myself and listened to Adele explain the artwork and what the symbols meant. He explained the *Eye of Horus*, and *The Senses,* and the *Weighing of Hearts in the Afterlife*. This was so bizarre because I had always looked on Google and sorts and tried to decipher these codes myself- but Adele seemed to leave out some of the details. I now believe it was because everyone must go on their own journey of sorts to discover this God given treasure, and they do so at different times in life. What I will say is that the artwork had even deeper meanings, and probably a lot more meaning than you or I will ever understand, Diary.

After explaining the *Eye of Horus* and the *Weighing of Hearts*, Adele took me into a dark room and showed me the art beneath the art. At this point I was again on cloud nine but in a calm way. I couldn't believe the natural high I was given from just seeing and learning about these things. Beneath the *Weighing of Hearts* there was an image of King Tut and a queen, I believe

Nefertiti. The images were now green and highlighted whereas the first images were golds, blacks, browns—your traditional Egyptian art colors. I couldn't believe it. The *Eye of Horus* hovered over an ancient Egyptian cat- and it too was shown in a fluorescent green. I was in disbelief. I now needed these pieces and Adel saw to it that I could obtain them. He gave me a deal, actually several. I was able to purchase both pieces for around $450 dollars. Normally one would think that I was just naive and had been hustled, but you would have just had to be on this journey with me to know it was by far not the case. As Adele and I discussed the artwork, Saber came back and asked if I wanted some coffee. I had been trying to stay away from coffee and drink tea, but my inner self said *you want that coffee*. He gave me a small clear glass, almost like a shot glass, and poured the coffee from a metal flask. It had no cream, possibly some sugar, but if I wasn't crazy, I would say it was just the way it tasted naturally. It was delicious and I had a couple of glasses during my experience there. So now I am almost $800 dollars in at this shop that I originally had no intention of going into. Yet again, we were not done.

Saber said he wanted to bring me to Abrahim, who dealt with healing and chakras. I was now in some sort of enchanting trance, unable to say no to anything and more importantly, I wanted to be healed. Saber said he could tell my heart had been broken recently. You would think that a marriage of 14 years would be the reason he saw this in me, and though my heart was broken, it was not a true love heart breaking like I felt about X. I only felt shame that I had given 14 years to this man

Bernard when in all honesty, he was cold and hurtful. At one point, he even asked me—while I was at my lowest and sickest, why I would not just go ahead and die.

Abrahim pulled out seven oils much like the first three that I had purchased from Saber. He said they were all in alignment with the seven chakras and showed me where to place each one and what to concentrate on for each area of the body all the way up to the crown chakra. When he pulled these out, I did not have my glasses on, so I was very pleased to see they were only a dollar or so each. After the conversation, while Saber and Abrahim bickered a bit back and forth in Egyptian, I noticed that the oils were actually $65 dollars apiece. I purchased them anyway, thankful, and grateful for the lesson. After this, Saber said that I needed to balance my heart- that my emotions were in a way uneven. It is strange because I remember feeling as though I didn't want my heart balanced. I enjoyed being by my-self, and I also enjoyed feeling true love for a man, even though this man was not actually present in the physical sense. I didn't want my heart (that I finally got back) to change even if it was some fantasy, but I let Saber listen to my heart. I cried, and he asked why... he sat there as if he could read my thoughts. He asked me when was the last time I spoke to X. It was embar-rassing to tell him that I had been forwarded to voicemail, and that every time I called X, he was anxious to get off the phone with me. Yet, I was still undeniably in love with this man. Saber told me that it was basically out of my hands, that I was beau-tiful, that I knew that I was beautiful, that I had to love myself, and that X was already gone. I didn't want to hear that. I was afraid after he listened to my heart that all of a sudden, my deep feelings of happiness just at the thought of being with X would go away. It scared me, but I also knew that if God wanted that, it would happen and I would still be okay. I cried and I told Saber that X and I were like brother and sister, and that I didn't realize when he was in my life that he may have really loved me as more than a friend. He asked if we had been intimate, and I told him I wouldn't really call it that– it was not making love, but we had connected. I told him that even after my desperate attempt of throwing myself at him while still married and on a business trip for music, that X still treated me as a friend, treated me as if nothing had changed. I told him I thought that X regretted being with me because I could not just be his. I was married, and married to an asshole, for lack of better words.

Saber again stressed to me that X was on his own journey, and that I needed to be on mine. He pulled out the *Weighing of Hearts* artwork and asked me how to spell my name. By the way, my name Nile is not really my name. Just like the Ting Tings state in their infamous song, *That's Not My Name*, I made up Nile just for you, Diary. Saber pulled out the Egyptian alphabet and each letter had one or two symbols attached to it. In short, he told me that based on my name, I was a giver, I loved arts and music, I wanted things right away in life, and there were more. But the one that rang the truest was that I was meant to be a lover. A hopeless romantic in a sense, that I was not built to be alone. This was eye opening and comforting, because society says a hopeless romantic is a fool more often than not. Society also tells everyone they *can* be alone, and women go around saying *I don't need a man,* but I think most of us do. It just needs to be the right man. I am a lover. I am now proud of this. I no longer look at it as a weakness after speaking with Saber.

Saber asked if we could go on a walk. He was shorter than me, but with kind eyes and an amazing energy, and if I didn't know better, he was flirting with me as we walked. Maybe trying to show me there was more to life than X. It didn't work. I only went home and fantasized that X was lying next to me, and the scary part is that this was after my heart had been evened out.

Before once again falling mentally hard for this man and doing something crazy like calling him again, I decided I was cute with my new hair, and more importantly, that I was hungry. Although I was determined to not make any desperate or unsafe decisions regarding going and partying in LA alone, I was hungry, and I felt the need to feel sexy and beautiful. It was refreshing because I needed praise from no one. So, I went to my apartment, and I got dressed up in tight black pants with a gold line down the side, a black lace bodysuit, and an MTV cropped black sweatshirt (my favorite of my most recent purchases). I put on some chunky black boots and went to a vegan restaurant called *Gratitude,* which was a mile or so away from where I was staying. I had a bowl of red bean chili with kale and had a small water and a pressed juice with coconut, pineapple, and ginger. It was pretty tasty. There was a man that sat a couple of seats down from the bar and he, like the ladies in the nail salon, asked me if I worked for MTV. I smiled both times and said

I wish. I told him that I got the sweatshirt at H&M in Colorado, and he asked if MTV was even still aired on cable. I told him I believed so.

After dinner, I was too cute to merely go back to the apartment, but I also wanted to be safe and stick to my instinct about not being stupid in LA. I decided to go to Sunset Boulevard, and you can bet I jammed the whole way there. I have always enjoyed driving and listening to music, but I don't just listen—I literally dance in my seat and I think my car feels the vibrations. While on Sunset bumpin' my music, I came across a street called Kings Road. It was a thin street that wound up a hill. At first, I thought that I was once again going the wrong direction down a one-way street. Thankfully I was not- the homes were absolutely phenomenal, and I could see why the street was named as it was. These homes were truly meant for kings, though I couldn't help but wonder after speaking to David (the man who checked me in) if the right kings lived there, or if it was once again proof that our system is unjust in its power. I remember thinking what on earth do these people do to be able to live in these amazing homes. Do they work, they must... Do they do what they love or are they slaves giving their energy away for a means of luxury? I couldn't help but think they must do what they love. I remember thinking how nice it would be to live there, even in a small room in one of those houses, but I also realized that sometimes less is more. I was perfectly content in my little apartment off the beach.

I drove back down the winding lane on Kings Road and saw all the white privileged young people laughing as they went to their entertainment for the night, looking as if they had not a care in the world. I wondered why power was so one sided.

I listened to rap and R&B on my drive back, came home and fell into a deep sleep after crying over regret for X.

Your Scene

Your eyes hunger for mine

But do you know?

Am I a game to you too

After so many games...

Now down to a few...

Will I ever see your face?

Do you need to see mine too?

I would say I am just crushing

But I think it is much more

Are you happy out there without me

Is there another person you adore?

When I look at your pictures at times

That is what it seems

But your eyes show me you hunger for much better things

Can I be part of your much better things?

Your bigger dreams?

Can our feet go back to sand?

Can I be a part of your better scene?

So many words I said

But clearly I didn't mean

The next morning, I arose with a feeling of gratefulness that I was able to be on this journey by myself. After going on a run along the beach, I pulled out my phone and went to the Duolingo app to practice more French. I had been learning it and had once asked Bernard to please learn it with me. He merely downloaded the app on his phone amongst many apps he had, but never took the time to speak it with me or learn it with me. As I imagined myself in France speaking a broken-down form of it (I was a beginner-beginner), I imagined being there with X and my daughters.

I then went to have breakfast. I ordered egg whites scrambled with roasted potatoes and a smoothie. I decided it was time to make another attempt at going to the Getty Museum.

The museum was unlike any other I have ever seen. The building itself was art. It was surrounded by trees and flowers all full in color, and it was set high up on a hill showing all the large California homes with their pools and guest houses. I was going to take the tram up to the gallery but was told I could walk by the security guard. It was a beautiful day, so I decided to walk. I wore a flowered sundress with sandals and a black and tan sun hat. I thought I looked particularly romantic, so I asked the security guard to take a photo of me. He did and I posted it on Instagram.

As I walked, I saw many couples holding hands and looking so in love. I somehow felt at peace being there alone. The walk to the museum was amazing and all I wanted to do was see the art inside. There were many exhibits, and I was anxious as to which ones to see first. There were older ladies at a desk giving a guided tour via a hand-held device. This device was like a phone and gave you information on each exhibit and the history behind it. I found it, quite frankly, annoying. I attempted to use it for a moment, and then decided I was perfectly capable of reading the inserts to the side of each art piece, which also gave you history, background, and details on the artist and their work.

I went to the NUDE Renaissance area incorporating ancient Roman art. Though beautiful, it was mostly filled with depictions of war, demigods, and white men looking as if it was their pleasure to slaughter people as long as they were in power. #FACTS— X used to say this when we instant messaged...facts.

After leaving that exhibit, I went to the "Three Religions Exhibit," which was quite an eye opener. It incorporated Islam, Catholicism, and Christianity. The art was amazing and the stories behind the art saddened me to the point of tears. There seemed to be an overwhelming recurring theme of stolen dreams and stolen love. There were images of black apostles and of a black Jesus. It was confusing, though, just as languages have been confused. The art was mixed up. For example, you would have black angels and Christ- like figures— mostly male, and then in the same image, a white woman or angel that was being held captive. I wondered if she too should have had dark skin, whether she be Mary, Ruth, or Eve herself. There were images of a boy with some form of a musical instrument, and one showed him tied to a tree. He seemed in every image to be searching for her. You know, X was a musician, too... I wept that day for him. I remember seeing a piece that showed a male and female being vetted by their very own angels for the night in which they would unite together as one physically. It was so romantic. I wondered why weddings and courtships weren't still like this today. It would prevent a lot of disease and it would make the wedding night or first time of union so special. As I looked on in awe at one piece, a beautiful black girl—maybe in her twenties, approached me, she was with a friend. She came up to me out of the blue and said that I looked so good standing and looking at the image I was looking at. She asked if I wanted a photo taken. I told her thank you, and overwhelmed at the compliment said, *"Yes, please!"*

My battery was low on my phone, and it died shortly after. I remember thinking to myself, I wish my best friend from middle school was here with me. Her name is Nicollette. I had not seen or spoken to her in years. I started to recall memories of our friendship. We sure had a good one. I remember that she was always sticking up for me. I recalled a time when someone (another black female) who was classically trained in dance, told me that I could not dance. I remember Nicollette literally fighting her for saying these simple words to me. I remember being in shock and feeling loved at the same time. Nicollette was thin and was just the cutest thing on the planet. She was one of those girls that could wear a paper bag with boots and look like she fell off of a runway. She was beautiful and one of the only true friends I have ever had. She, ironically enough, met

Bernard as her and I's relationship started to disintegrate. I recall telling her that I was going to marry him one day, and Nicollette had simply replied, *"I don't think that's a good idea."* Like a ghost, the thought that I should have listened to her haunted me at that moment.

I wanted Nicollette back in my life. Her brother had died, and he was a special one as well. Calvin had the best smile, and he and Nicollette were the first to turn me on to one of my favorite songs. If you have not heard it, Diary, it is called *Tender Love* and was recorded by Force MDS. I very much regretted not going to the funeral and not reaching out to her like I should have. It was as if I was under some sort of Bernard curse, and I was completely intoxicated with trying to make this white man and his family happy. When all along, Nicollette, Calvin and Wanita, their mom, had truly always been my family. Bernard, the person I was consumed with above anything and everyone, didn't care to love me the way I needed to be loved or the way I tried to love him, even when my heart did not agree with loving him. It made me very mad. If I had emojis on my laptop, the angry orange emoji with the word F##^ word would be inserted here. In any event, Diary, by the time I reached out to Nicollette I got a call back from her mom and she said she would give the message for Nicollette to call me. I never heard anything back, but I don't blame her. I just knew I missed her presence in my life.

What I Like, No- Love About You

Your eyes

Your skin

Your chin

Your waves

Your heart at its best

Your rhythm

Your craft

Your energy

Your math

Your eyes you must know

Are the windows to my soul

A year? A month?

No longer counting by days

You are both out of reach

Yet I still hear words that you say

Through nature and music and my own heart's pain

Your friendship and love

I long to regain

Please come back to me

As Janet once sang

I was not expecting to cry at the museum, but after literally weeping in the Religions exhibit, I took out my phone to call my sister. I was now in a garden setting that blew my mind with its beauty. When my sister picked up, I began telling her how much this garden reminded me of what the Garden of Eden must have looked like in a smaller form. It had every herb and flower you could imagine. It was in the shape of a circle and the trees were so colorful, the flowers so in bloom. There were water features and it felt like I was in heaven. Now coming from someone who has pretty much tried every recreational drug known to man, for the first time in a long time I was on a natural high. I felt as one with God.

Eventually, I tried to find my way back to the entrance where you exit the Museum to get on the tram, but instead found myself going down a staircase that led to the most beautiful trail I had ever seen. I immediately saw two deer below where I was standing, and just began to walk on the trail. It was a sight to be seen. As I walked, I felt God with me, and even crazier, I felt X with me in a spiritual sort of way. I began imagining that he was literally there with me, enjoying the views that I was enjoying. I remember telling him all the things we could see and do together if he would just allow me to love him, to just give me a chance now that I was not with Bernard. I remember telling God that our people should be the ones living in the large houses on the hills. I recall a voice coming to me and asking, *which home would you pick for us?* I began to smile a smile like no other as I stated, *well gee- they are all sufficient.* But I was up for the task, and after looking at several homes, I finally was able to narrow it down to three. One was a gray home with hues of green and lots of contemporary glass windows, and a sparkling shining pool in the backyard. The second home was a white stucco, and it looked like something out of France. It was smaller than the first house, but quite stunning. The last one, the one I decided on, was also made of white stucco finished with a Spanish tiled roof, and that is the one I settled on. I didn't stop here however, I told God all of my thoughts on how the world could be a better place. I told God that the art made me sad, and that I felt that an evil force or evil people were in charge, and that again the power was misplaced, even stolen. I felt God was listening to me. At that point, I even wondered if X was my god. As I walked for two hours or more, I ended up picking out houses not just for me, the girls and X, but also for my mom, X's mom, my sister, my brother, Nicole, her son Isaac, and a couple of X's friends that I had met previously. I know I sound like a silly girl in high school at this point, but isn't that the best kind of love, after all?

I got lost on the trail in trying to find my way back to the Museum and the exit—I walked up and down stairs, but none led to the exit. In my previous mental state, drugs, or no drugs, I would have been very uncomfortable and certainly in a fit of rage at this point. I remember being grateful for my sobriety and the fact that I was as calm as a cucumber and, as stated in the movie *Strictly Business*, I was just as sharp as a tack. I was in bliss, and I felt connected.

As I asked God to lead me back to the exit of the museum, I saw that there were two ways I could have gone after walking for a couple of hours. I was at this point ready to find the way back. There was a plane in the sky going right- I went that way and *voila,* I finally reached my destination to exit the museum. I walked back down in lieu of taking the tram- made it to my car only to realize that I had left the annoying tour guide device in my purse. I walked back up to the museum to drop it off in exchange for my ID, and then took the tram back down. My legs had gotten quite a workout on this day.

I came back to my apartment and changed into something comfortable. I went down to the beach and cried because of the art that I saw and the overwhelming experience I had on the walk at the museum was still with me. I felt cleansed again after my cry. Once I got back to my room, my brother sent me a song called *Love Me in Whatever Way* by James Blake. It was one of the most beautiful songs I had heard in a long time. It made me want to write song lyrics again. I used to write them effortlessly, and I had been writing as of late due to completely losing my way. Moreso, it made me think of a boy I met once, the first boy I ever kissed.

His name was Frog- my family was living in Denver and my mom had moved us there. My dad was to follow us from Atlanta, but never did. We lived in a place called High Hollows, and I met Frog there. One day, a group of us decided we were going to act in a play. We decided on Romeo and Juliet. Frog was Romeo and I was Juliet. I remember kissing him and feeling him erect through his jeans. I remember being traumatized because I was too young. I was maybe nine years old. We moved after this to a different community as my mom didn't think High Hollows was a good neighborhood. I don't blame her because one night, my sister and I were out walking, and a bullet grazed my sister's ear. It didn't touch it, but it was loud, and we felt its wind. I now found myself thinking about this kiss, about stolen love, and about X and the possibility that he was Frog. That he was someone who had protected and loved me from afar all these years. I thought about one of the few Disney movies with black characters, the *Princess and the Frog*. I thought about how much I loved X no matter who he was. As I thought more and more of the possibilities of a true romance, a voice inside my head told me to go outside. I had promised Saber that I would walk up to the Santa Monica pier where there was a ferris wheel lit up with lights that one could see from all the way down the beach apartment where I was staying. As I walked in my sweats and tennis shoes, I played the song my brother sent me, and a track list began to play that mirrored this song. All were romantic—some blunt and sexual, and I felt as if I was walking to the soundtrack of our romance through the years up to present day. As I walked to the carnival, I felt at a crossroads in life. I felt that I had been betraying myself—doing things that society said were best when in all actuality, I was killing myself on the inside. I thought about how I wanted this cycle to stop, that I did not want my daughters repeating this insanity, and that I physically could not bear it any longer at the age of 38. Before, when walking on the boardwalk, I noticed many single people or groups of friends in threes or fives, but this night as I played the soundtrack in my ears, I only noticed the stars above me and couples passing by hand in hand. I remember thinking to myself, *Bernard never held me or touched me as these men were touching and holding the women by their sides.* Somehow, I didn't crumble and fall, somehow, I was ready to see the romance and boy did I see it. As the soundtrack played, I walked up the boardwalk and felt as if I was in an enchanted new world. Every couple that walked by reminded me of what X and I could have been.

One of my favorite drinks as a kid was cherry ices. The pier had many rides and many food booths. I stopped at one of them and got a veggie burger and a cherry icy. As I waited for the burger, I felt like I was in a land of teenage fever. The couples were of all ages, but they all seemed so in love. In love with each other's perfection and imperfections. They all seemed so warm and cozy. Although at this point, I should have felt jaded regarding Bernard's blatant lack of love for me, I only thought of who was turning out to be my true love—reciprocated or not. I did recall a time or several times where I would wake up in my old room with Bernard, and I would be genuinely happy to start the day. Thinking that the days—as monotonous as they were, would still bring joy. We had cats, and I remember so many times feeling envious of them because Bernard would kiss them and snuggle with them as if he were in love; yet I would not even get a good morning or a look of anything. If I did get a glance, it was regularly one of contempt and hate.

The veggie burger was good, but it was not my favorite. I realized that food doesn't always have to taste good. X told me this once, and I remember looking at him cross eyed as we laughed over the phone. Now I realized two things—being a vegan was going to take time and some getting used to, and X was so much smarter than I ever gave him credit for.

After stopping to look at the ocean waves on the pier, I headed back to my apartment and began thinking about all the times women in my life would say, *I can do bad all by myself.* Whether they were talking about their own current nightmare relationships or trying to give me advice about my own, I thought about how I would have loved myself alone so much more if I wasn't trying to love a man incapable of loving me back the way I needed to be loved. The sad thing is, Bernard was a very intelligent man, it's not as if he was incapable of love. I realized at that moment that he didn't feel I deserved his love- he didn't want to love me as I needed to be loved. Almost as if he got off on hurting me, dangling just enough to make me stay.

Bernard was notorious for dangling carrots in my face. In regard to travel, wants, and dreams in life, decorations I wanted to purchase for our home, Bernard always made it out as if it was a crime to have anything, even though we both made good money, and in fact, I often doubled or tripled his salary, still he always said no. It was odd because his parents were both well off, his brother had a rental property and a new home on land. Yet, me and my daughters often went without our basic needs met—I had no nice underwear, for example. I would occasionally get a pair—never for my birthday or holidays, and I would always buy them for myself. But I would go years with the same under garments, and he cared not one bit. The girls he did love (and to a point where it backfired on me) and as he could do no wrong in their eyes, when he and I would fight, I was normally both the odd one out and the bad guy. I felt ganged up on by him and worst of all, by my own little seeds. Never give a man that much control, especially if he isn't the one.

The world or society will tell you that there is no such thing as a romantic love or a true love, and that we marry and we accept each other for better or for worse, but that the love fades. I do believe we must nurture and work to keep the love growing, but I now do not believe the above statements of society to be true. It's actually quite sad if you think about it. I was literally accepting no love thinking this is what everyone does, who am I to want better? Betraying my heart, the entire time. The heart is only treacherous when we betray it repeatedly.

Past Lovers

So many words written out of heartache and longing for true love

When I think back and look back at the torn pages

The books thrown to trash

I recall some of the words

I recall chards of glass

I wonder if they were all just pre-colors yeah pre hues

Past lovers guiding my words

Words only really meant for you

Please tell me that it's true

That time really does heal all

Please tell me it's not such a bad thing

When you finally decide to fall

Please help me see the difference

In hope, and what is real

Sometimes I think to let this thing go

It's just I finally know how to feel

As I got closer to my room, I met a man named Cornbread on the pier. He just so happened to be selling candy, one of which was my favorite. They were sour punch straws, likely toxic but very addictive. I only had large bills on me, and I did not have a dollar. I asked if he could break a hundred-dollar bill and likely insulted him. He said no but said that he was always up and pointed to a hut-like structure overlooking the pier. He said that he cooked for homeless people and helped the poor even though looking at him, I wondered how he could be so generous when he, too, looked as if he struggled. I thanked him for fronting the candy to me and told him I would come back and pay him tomorrow. As I walked away from him, I remember thinking that I should have just given him the hundred-dollar bill. He was helping others. It was the least I could do. The next morning, I found the hut and I left the one-hundred-dollar bill with his nephew, who held the same box of candy in his hands.

After leaving the hut, I was in a ball of total excitement. It was Sunday, the day of the super blood wolf moon lunar eclipse. I no longer felt scared like I did on the first day when I called my sister, but more so anxious for the hour to arrive. I went down to the ocean, spoke to it more, begged that it heard my prayers involving reconnecting with my daughters and reconnecting with my best friend and with my true love. I didn't feel silly talking to the ocean about these things, but more so felt it necessary no matter whether it seemed doable or not. I asked the ocean to connect with the moon and sun tonight. I don't know everything, hell hardly anything, but I knew that this eclipse was going to be special, and that I needed my prayers to be heard. The ocean had listened to me—I could tell by the waves. I felt connected to it and asked that it carry my prayers to exactly what was occurring with me.

I went back outside around 8pm, and the eclipse had already started. I felt total and utter amazement as I looked up in the sky and saw the beautifully lit moon with a small disk shadowing it above. One was the sun, the other the moon. I had heard before that you should not look upon eclipses. That could be the case with only solar eclipses, but I had now looked upon both. One that occurred a couple of years prior to my visit here, and the other I was looking at right now. I could not take my eyes off it. It brought about a song in my mind, *The Blower's Daughter* by Damien Rice. It was so amazing and so beautiful. My legs grew weary from standing. I knew it was likely from all the energy I was taking in with my own two eyes. I walked back up to my room, grabbed a blanket and pillow and went to the balcony.

The balcony had many plants and flowers that hung over the boardwalk below along with a huge surfboard. I had an organic ice cream sandwich that I purchased from Whole Foods up the street earlier. I laid down staring at the interaction between the sun and the moon. I felt a strong sensation that my prayers in regard to my girls and X had not only been heard but were being answered, part of me felt like they were going to be answered immediately. The other part of me knew deep down that I needed to pray for patience. One thing I do know is that this night brought me no anxiety in regard to money, which state I was going to call home, X, my girls, my desires to work, or anything else. It was just me and the celestial bodies. I did fall asleep imagining that I was in X's arms. In the past I always touched myself and came instantly, as in three minutes max, and I typically did it in some degrading form or fashion. Whether it was me picturing Bernard with other women or porn, it was actually quite disturbing. Now, I could touch myself all night thinking of X and in multiple ways. I was the happiest woman on the planet, yet he was not there. It was just my fantasies of him, and they were enough and more potent than any physical encounter with Bernard or any other man I had ever been with.

"8"

He controlled me when I was blind

You taught me when I could finally see

But when will we be my love?

When will we be?

I don't feel I am meant to be here

Can you tell me are you just like me?

If so, when will we be?

If so, when will we be?

I see all that you have done

Is it really from you to me?

If so, when will we be?

If so, when will we be?

Have I been bitten to the point of no return?

Is my sacrifice no you and me?

I am just trying to overstand

Why I feel you but you I can't see

Am I dead in love?

Is this my everlasting dream?

If so, can you please change it to the physical you and me?

I woke up Monday morning to an undeniable sentence that came to mind. It was more so a question that asked, *"Do I have to write you an entire book or album before you will speak to me again?"* I got ready that morning listening to X's album, and I knew that he was talking not only about me, but to me. It had inspired me to write down my overwhelming feelings for him once again. This time the title was a simple infinity sign... A lateral 8.

"Infinity" ∞

I am so in love with you

I've never been in love like this

Actually, I don't think I have ever truly been in love

After feeling like this

You have my soul, my heart, you have my only kiss

I want it with you

God, how much can one miss?

I love you so much because you saw me

I love you so much, without you here, without your touch in the physical

Yet you hold me close in the mental

Writing this poem made me recall several things about how I had lied to myself in my 14-year sham of a marriage. I recall the time I looked at Bernard's phone early on in our marriage, thinking all was well, but I just had a feeling that he was up to something. I was not one who considered myself to be jealous or untrusting, yet I always felt threatened in our relationship. I went on his phone and saw a Facebook message. He had reached out to an old high school crush by the name of Jenny. As I am reading this message he sent to her, my blood started to boil, and I was in a rage. The message said that he was wondering how long she had been with her boyfriend and that he had been thinking of her, and often. She replied, *"We have been together for a couple of years"* and *"aren't you married, Bernard?"* To which he replied, *"I am married, but we are getting a divorce."* She then stated, *"Oh my gosh- that's horrible- divorces are horrible."* The bastard replied, *"No, no trust me it's a great thing in this case."*

I threw Bernard's phone at him in a psychotic rage and told him that us divorcing was news to me. You know what the funny thing is? It took the man six years to apologize for doing this. I would throw it up in his face over the following years because I just couldn't believe him, nor did I trust him any longer. He said that so what, he reached out to an old friend when we were not getting along too well. Again, this was news to me.

I recalled the time when we first started dating and got snowed in. I made him breakfast the next day. Now let's get something straight right now- it became a running joke with Bernard's friends every time we saw them, they would ask...*so did you guys finally do it?* You see, I fell asleep—not just any sleep, but literally a coma-like sleep every time that he and I would try and connect sexually when we first started dating. So, although we fooled around on this snowed-in weekend, it was as if God himself said *DON'T LET THIS MAN ENTER YOUR TREASURE.* We did everything but connect physically. Anyway, I made him breakfast the next morning and I accidentally burnt the toast. Stay tuned for my next reading entitled 'BURNT TOAST, Diary, because you see, this should have been my clue to leave, dude. To not allow anything to make me settle for a man who was just cooked breakfast by me on our first overnight date, to then immediately make me feel like crap by rudely yelling at me, "*YOU BURNT THE TOAST, and I don't have a job, I don't have any money, you wasted two pieces of bread.*" Yes, Diary, I know—put me to shame now. Even writing this and reading it out loud, I feel disgusted that I ever gave him a second chance. I did not talk to him for a few days after that, but I let him back into my life just to spend fourteen years with this asshole, and to experience hurt like no other for someone who was basically treating me like a joke for our entire marriage. It made me think of X, how opposite the two were, and even more so how alike X and I were. How we were meant to be.

Fall

"He made me weak

He made me want him without a touch

without a call

with a mere Insta -Gram post

I felt destined to be with him

not in the form of desperation like society would think

in the form of desperation to complete myself and the

love that I knew he too felt for me

words were not needed

the feeling said it all

it was meant to be

it was meant to call

God was in fact involved

I wasn't stupid

I was just called to fall"

I flashed back to a time after leaving Bernard where I was desperate for money, and we had owned our home for over ten years and had a very large sum of equity in it. Technically, I owned the home for eight of those ten years and had at the last minute decided to add Bernard to the title. It was a very bad decision. Even before splitting up, I had to beg him to take out a home equity loan so that I could try and fix up our very old home. The windows were leaking when it rained, the doors were broken and cracked, the filters were often dirty, I wanted a claw foot tub which was not allowed in his eyes as it was not "practical." I wanted to get new furniture as we had the same couch set for ten years and the main couch was broken. The girls had also requested this- when they had friends over, they would comment on how they were embarrassed. I am not one who is materialistic, and if you don't have the money, that is one thing. I, too, believe often that less is more. But when you work like a dog and make twice the amount that your EX-husband did along with him making a decent amount of money, this is a form of financial prison and control. I finally was able to convince him to pull out $40,000 and I was so excited to be able to finally update my kitchen and get some new things when Bernard decided that we were just going to pay off credit card debt. I was under a spell of mind control. When I finally broke from the spell, I now have to battle him to split our equity. My equity in reality. Enough about him right now. I just can't believe the time I've wasted.

Saturn

"Teardrops were falling on Saturn's rings

With my icy cold hands in my head

Remember that last day

you screamed at me

Well that's the day that I chose him instead"

Wonder:

We met in a broken public

Something kinda tragic, and lovesick

We still had the fire burning in our eyes...

He said that he loved me on the first day

And I was thinking he was in a bad place

So, I said it back

But I didn't lie

We said that we would never break our chain

Putting it simply he was more than vain

But I had the trust

I didn't wonder why

So, at this point, it probably seems like I am a love-struck teenager with yet another spell of sorts, and honestly that could be. One spell with a white man that did not give a damn about me, and now one with a black man I want to be my King who behaves as if he doesn't give a damn about me.

We are taught to respect ourselves as women, but I ask you, do we? Am I even respecting myself giving my heart to someone who won't even return my calls? It seems like I have been so happy at the thought of someone, yet I cry so much. I cry tears of joy, regret, and tears of sadness, wondering still why I am not good enough for even a phone call. Yet, I still feel more loved than I ever felt with Bernard or anyone else. Maybe I am just in love with myself. I ask myself if X knows magic of sorts, to where he, too, cursed me with a love spell. I feel I was only good enough for part of his spirit but not his flesh. At times, either way, I feel it is messed up. I still love him, but I still hurt. When I try to think of breaking away from X, not touching myself, not thinking about him, not noticing his posts or photos in hopes of reconnecting with him again, it makes me so sad, and I guess I can't figure out which is worse for my soul. One of his songs had a piece of a speech from Martin Luther King Jr. and it said you must love completely because it is lovely to love, and that you must do it honestly because it is right to be honest. I am so torn right now, Diary. Torn. Some say God is a woman. *Hmmmm.* Whether man or woman, I can't help but feel that he or she wants me to want what I want and who I want. I deserve it, and God agrees. It has been engraved into my heart. To betray the heart is to die.

Is it all a lie? All of it? What do you do when you are at a cross-roads? You love yourself more than you have ever loved yourself, but you must love God, too. You must listen to what God tells you. *The Lord works in mysterious ways,* they say. Today I feel that to be very true. I don't know everything, but sometimes I feel as simple of a human being that I am, God should be even more simple. I promised that no matter what, I would be honest with you, Diary. So, I will continue to be. Please don't judge me.

Boys to Men

You say your eyes are really open

You say it's me you really see

Well if that's the case

Then walk away from them to me

I never meant to get this close to you
I'm often sorry that I did

You got me feelin' like some schoolgirl

Just like some broken-hearted kid

You say your eyes are really open

You say I'm all you ever see

But I just don't believe you baby

'Cuz men are where they want to be

It was a lovely and sunny Monday morning. I went on a run and came back to the apartment very hungry. On my run I listened to Nicki Minaj and Migos. I was so happy on my run that I would literally stop mid-run to dance in the sun. I did not care who saw me. I just cared about being happy. I went down to the ocean and thanked it for having mercy on me. I thanked the ocean for listening to me.

I looked online for vegan soul food and was shocked when a restaurant called *My Two Cents* pulled up. What shocked me was the amazing photos showing all sorts of tasty looking soul food. It was about a forty-minute drive, but I needed to go there. I went to the restaurant, which was tucked into a small shopping center. The restaurant was quaint with a large personality. There were two young black gentlemen greeting guests behind the counter. The counter itself was a painting to look upon. I saw so many delicious looking cakes and cobblers. My eyes were about to pop out of my head in excitement. Both young men at the counter were so nice. Hip Hop music played, and the environment felt alive. It was my favorite place out of all the restaurants that I had experienced in Los Angeles so far. I was given a menu and was somewhat anxious about what to order. I remember my eyes being guided directly to a spicy vegan spaghetti—yes vegan spaghetti made at a soul food restaurant. I ordered it immediately as I felt like God wanted me to taste it.

Oh my gosh, boy was I thankful that God did. It was not only the best vegan dish that I had eaten since becoming vegetarian /low key vegan, it was the BEST spaghetti I have ever had in my entire life. The spaghetti sat in a brown sauce with green, yellow, and red bell peppers, onions, greens, and tomatoes. In addition, there were pieces of vegan meat that legitimately tasted like Italian sausage. I ordered a lemonade to go along with it, and it was served with a single piece of mint. It was so good. The atmosphere was loud but exciting. The chef cooked in the back and always came out to greet and say goodbye to the guests eating there. For a first timer, this was an adrenaline rush. After my lunch, I looked at the dessert counter and noticed peach cobbler—southern peach cobbler, one of my all-time favorites. I ordered a piece for myself even though I felt somewhat bad as it was not a vegan peach cobbler. It was, however, delicious, and I told myself that I deserved this piece of peach cobbler and that I was going to eat it in peace. Before leaving, I told the chef that her spaghetti was absolutely fantastic, and I truthfully wanted to lick the plate. I also warned her that I would likely be back again that same evening or the following day. She was very pleasant and thankful.

My new and cute weave was starting to become a problem. No one warned me how itchy weaves could be. I decided that I should have dumped an entire thing of Crisco Oil on my head before getting it done. I ended up scratching half of the stitching off my head in aggravation of the itch. I called Gloria to request another appointment immediately and met with Tonya once again. She added some oil to my hair this go round and added some fake hair at the bottom since I was naturally rocking a mohawk that was very short at the bottom. It was not nearly as itchy this time. I thanked Tonya again, tipped her and decided it was close enough to dinner for me to start look-ing for a good restaurant. I settled on an Ethiopian restaurant that sat in a marketplace amongst other small shops. I wore casual green Adidas leggings with a green half top that stated "troublemaker's club" in bold letters. The restaurant was quaint yet crowded. I waited for about twenty minutes before being seated. When I sat down, I was greeted by a waitress with long black hair and dark eyes. She spoke Ethiopian and was very at-tractive. She gave me a menu and then went to refill drinks for the table of five that sat across from me. As I sipped on my wa-ter and looked over the menu, I noticed the table of five as their food was served to them. They were eating very large raw red cubes of meat ...yes red as in bloody and seemed to be delight-ed in eating this dish uncooked. I was unsure as to what meat it was, but it did not look attractive to me and turned my stom-ach as I saw them intake this meat. I ordered my vegetarian meal which consisted of greens, a flat cornbread, and black-eyed peas. I ordered a lemonade and ate quietly. As I ate there, a young man with an X on his hat came with two friends and sat down at the table next to me. They seemed to be having a very interesting conversation. I remember thinking this as they were just young men. The gentlemen were in their twenties, and mostly spoke to each other about the system and social in-justices. I remember not being able to take my eyes off the guy with the X hat. Not because I wanted to get to know him but because the X made me think of well, you guessed it... X.

After eating my dinner, I asked a young man where the re-strooms were. He showed me and waited outside the restroom for me to come out. He asked if I was from California. He asked me for my number. He was a very attractive Ethiopian man and appeared to be my same age. I told him I was taken. As I walked to my car that night, I felt good about the lie I had just told. I played "*A Boogie Wit the Hoodie*" on my car drive back to my apartment. I felt good. I felt so good, in fact, that I went to my room to immediately touch myself while thinking of X. When I finished about an hour or so later, I went for a walk on the beach. As I came out of my apartment building, I heard rap music playing. I saw a single black man with a boombox and a mic rapping the lyrics, "*We did it in Venice.*" I blushed as I had just got done masturbating in thought of X. The gentleman did not stop there. He then proceeded to shout me out. "*Hey lady in the green! You look dope. Green is now my favorite color,*" he said enthusiastically. I blushed again as I reached down to put a ten-dollar bill in his tip jar. I asked the man for his name. He stated his name was Artist. We smiled at one another and then I went to walk further down the beach. As I left his presence, I heard the lyrics freedom bursting from his mouth.

Venice Connection

We did it in Venice :)

We did it in Venice:)

Rare

The hardest piece is the feeling smart

Is it building me up or simply tearing me apart?

My heart, My Heart

Well it wants what it wants

But my mind cries out stop

From all of the head taunts

My head cries out go

And pleads let this man know

That you are too rare

For one to haunt to and fro

I wondered what it would be like to go from shore to shore playing music as Artist did.

He seemed so cool, happy and at peace with life. It made me think of the feeling I get when I write. Writing, whether it be books I feel that no one will read, or songs I feel that no one will hear, poetry, my songs turned to poetry when in my heart I knew they were so much more.

I opened my apartment and laid down. I started to have a panic attack in regard to the girls, going back home or staying in California. I told myself, I am not too old to live my dreams. I told myself I was capable of anything. I reminded myself of the book I referenced at the beginning, Diary. I prayed to God at that moment because I didn't know what to do about my new hopes of living in California with the girls. As I lay on the bed sobbing like a little girl, tears fell from my eyes and hit my cell phone. My tears must have caused pressure against the phone because my pictures of my apartment in Colorado pulled up, and it was as if God heard my prayer and instantly answered it for me. My apartment was so cute. The girls had finally gotten settled there. I took in a deep breath and sighed. As I lay there, Diary, I was finally content to go home and was finally getting to a point where it didn't matter whether I ever saw or spoke to X again. I laid there that night wishing I had five bottles of wine. I cried myself to sleep in the thought of letting X go, but I also knew that as Saber had stated, *if God wanted it to be, it would be.* I slept surprisingly well that night, eager to wake up and head back home to Colorado.

The next morning, I woke up and put some coffee on. I started to pack up after stepping out to the balcony to take in the view of the ocean again. I decided that I needed to do one more run down the beach and have one more heart to heart with the ocean. I threw on some gray wide legged sweatpants that I had purchased on one of my many shopping sprees here in California. I accompanied the pants with a Fred Siegel t-shirt that read "Intuition," and my new Adidas tennis shoes. The run was nice, refreshing. It was about 67 degrees outside. I ran down the pier and listened to *Mind Over Matter* by Young the Giant. I then listened to *Planez* by Jeremih, and the strangest thing happened as my feet twisted in the sand. I looked out to the ocean and my body felt so free, it was as if I began to fly over the water. I was physically grounded, but my mind was free from any, and all fear. Whether X and I would get together, I didn't care, though I still danced in wonder and hope at the thought of him one day coming into my life again. I felt no fear of the world, not in the aspect of my daughters' love. They loved me because I gave birth to them and raised them. I had no fear of work or money. I felt God with me and was at peace that I was now living in a language that God and I both understood.

The Bet

Placed a bet

You'd love me too...

But how dare you...

Go and leave it all so cold

Why would I ever sink into your soul?

X Games

Taking people out in my dreams for you.

I got all types of extremes for you.

Proof For Saturn

We killed the whole world

Baby, me and you...

Buried them alive

And guess what

I got the proof

We Killed the whole world

baby me and you

Nails into their coffins

Just so we could cut loose

Trust

You are but a mystery

My bones break well

They do ...

To your intensity

No one can explain

It's true but makes no sense to me

Why you are what you are

The brightest of all the stars

You're a wonder

that's what you are

Without seeing without speaking to the other

We communicate though it can often shade our summer

So until that day my wonder

You are but a wonder

And instead of being frightened

I look ..well

forward to your thunder

And I wonder ...

Do you feel the same trust

If you don't it's okay

I feel it for the both of us

Did you hear that the same way?

I said enough for the both of us

I said enough for the both of us

And when it's time maybe we will

Fall upon something heavenly

Like hell, maybe some stardust

So for now if you lack trust

If you want to give up

If you trip and get stuck

I'll love you my wonder

I said until it's enough for the both of us

Silent

He came and talked to me

As usual, was silent

He came and crossed the line

As I was feeling violent

You'll never make it if you don't learn how to breathe
child

You'll never make it if not in love with your own wild style

Until next time diary...

THE END

Destiny Kimble

Destiny Kimble is a poet, musician, writer, and travel enthusiast. She enjoys art, nature, reading, music, and family. Her daughters are her true inspiration in all she does.